16.00

SAM AND DASHER

Rookie reader

BY
CHARNAN SIMON

ILLUSTRATED BY
GARY BIALKE

Children's Press®

A Division of Grolier Publishing

New York   London   Hong Kong   Sydney
Danbury, Connecticut

FOR THE REAL DASHER
AND HIS WONDERFUL PEOPLE-
TOM, JEANNE, JAMIE, COLIN, T.J.,
RYAN, AND TIERNEY MARIE
-C. S.

FOR DEREK,
THE CANTANKEROUS
WALLABY THAT LIVES
UNDER MY PORCH
-G. B.

READING CONSULTANT
LINDA CORNWELL
LEARNING RESOURCE CONSULTANT
INDIANA DEPARTMENT
OF EDUCATION

Library of Congress Cataloging-in-Publication Data
Simon, Charnan.
Sam and Dasher / by Charnan Simon ; illustrated by Gary Bialke.
p. cm. — (A rookie reader)
Summary: When next-door neighbor dogs Dasher and Sam start to visit back and forth by ripping a screen, Sam's
owner Rosie solves the problem by putting in a doggie door.
ISBN 0-516-20702-4 (lib. bdg.)   0-516-26252-1 (pbk.)
[1. Dogs—Fiction. 2. Neighbors—Fiction.]
I. Bialke, Gary, ill. II. Title. III. Series.
PZ7.S6035Saj 1997
[E] —dc21
96-40361
CIP
AC

Rosie's dog Sam had lots of friends.

His best friend, Dasher,

lived right next door.

Sam and Dasher played chase.

They played tug-of-rope.

They played
wrestle in the mud.

Sam loved Dasher. Dasher loved Sam.

One day, Sam was bored.

Then the best thing happened.

Dasher came over to play,

all by himself!

17

Sam was so happy!

Rosie was not.

The next day, Sam went to see Dasher

all by himself.

Sam was so happy!

Rosie was not.

The third day, Sam and Dasher
played chase all over the place.

Rosie was still not happy.

But she was smart.

And she loved Sam.

Now everyone was happy.

ABOUT THE AUTHOR

Charnan Simon lives in Madison, Wisconsin, with her husband, Tom Kazunas, her daughters, Ariel and Hana, and the real Sam. This Sam is part collie and part golden retriever, and he really does have a best friend named Dasher.

One summer, Sam and Dasher took out a number of screens in their eagerness to play together. This was when they were teenagers. Today, they know better, and they wait politely at the door for their people to let them in and out.

ABOUT THE ILLUSTRATOR

Gary Bialke lives in Portland, Oregon, where it just plain rains way more than it really needs to. With four dogs runnir around the house, that's a lot of muddy feet. In retrospect, he thinks that mayb just one **ENORMOUS** mutt would have been a better idea.

Gary enjoys amateur dog-sled racing drawing in books, and working on his animal-shaped hat collection.